FERGUS AND ZEKE

AND THE FIELD DAY CHALLENGE

KATE MESSNER

ILLUSTRATED BY HEATHER ROSS

CANDLEWICK PRESS

FOR MY AMAZING EDITOR, ANDREA,
AND HER FAVORITE READERS, KAREN AND MAXINE
K. M.

FOR EVERYONE AT PECK SLIP SCHOOL
H. R.

Text copyright © 2020 by Kate Messner
Illustrations copyright © 2020 by Heather Ross

Candlewick Sparks®. Candlewick Sparks is a registered trademark of Candlewick Press, Inc.

First paperback edition 2022

Library of Congress Catalog Card Number 2020902242
ISBN 978-1-5362-0202-1 (hardcover)
ISBN 978-1-5362-2360-6 (paperback)

22 23 24 25 26 27 CCP 10 9 8 7 6 5 4 3 2 1

Printed in Shenzhen, Guangdong, China

This book was typeset in Minion.
The illustrations were created digitally.

Candlewick Press
99 Dover Street
Somerville, Massachusetts 02144

www.candlewick.com

CONTENTS

CHAPTER 1

MICE IN TRAINING

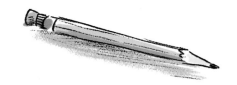

FERGUS AND ZEKE always had fun in Miss Maxwell's room. They did everything the children did.

When it was time for science, they conducted experiments.

When it was art time, they sculpted with clay.

And when it was time for gym, Fergus and Zeke did their exercises.

One day, Miss Maxwell told the class, "Tomorrow will be our school field day. We will have lots of outdoor fun. There will be games and contests and races. Look!" She pointed out the window. "Ms. Khan is outside now, getting things ready. This afternoon, we'll go out to see what the events will be!"

After lunch, the children lined up to go outside. Fergus and Zeke hitched a ride in Emma's backpack. They wanted to see what was happening, too!

Ms. Khan, the gym teacher, was spreading a big plastic tarp on the playground. "This is for the waterslide," she said.

Next, Ms. Khan marked a course with bright orange flags. "That is for our relay race," she said.

Ms. Khan set up bars for the high jump, limbo, and hurdles. Then she unloaded a big box from her pickup truck.

"What's in there?" asked Neela.

"Lots of things," Ms. Khan said. "Potato sacks for our potato sack race. Hula-Hoops for the Hula-Hoop contest. Ropes for the tug-of-war. Balloons for our water balloon toss. And a big, bright parachute for our parachute game. At the end of the day, we'll all go inside for ice pops."

"Wow!" said Emma. "I'm going to jump the highest of all!"

"I'm going to win the Hula-Hoop contest!" said Will.

"I can't wait to go on the waterslide and eat ice pops!" said Lucy.

"I can't wait for everything!" said Neela.

Fergus and Zeke felt the same way.

While the children finished their after-noon work, Fergus and Zeke got ready for field day.

They practiced jumping over hurdles . . .

and running on their spinny wheel.

They stretched to prepare for the limbo
contest . . .

and did exercises so they'd be extra strong
for tug-of-war.

At the end of the day, Miss Maxwell told her class, "Eat a good dinner and get plenty of sleep tonight. You want to be well rested in the morning!"

Fergus and Zeke ate their sunflower seeds, but they were almost too excited to sleep. Field day was going to be amazing!

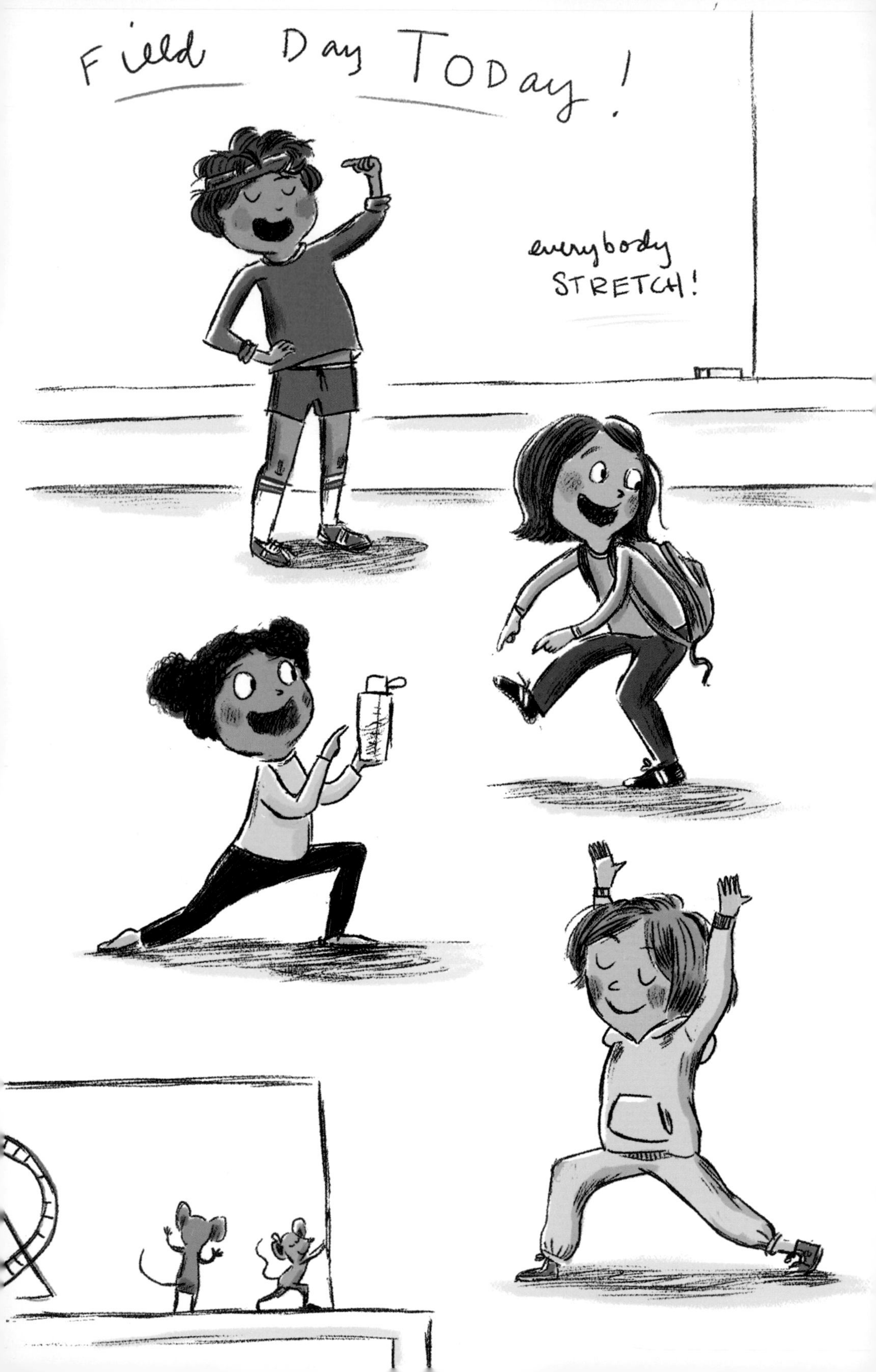
Field Day TODay!
everybody STRETCH!

CHAPTER 2
TOO SMALL

The next day, everyone arrived at school early. Miss Maxwell's class was very excited.

"I brought my favorite water bottle," said Neela.

"I am wearing my super-fast sneakers," said Emma.

"I've got my lucky headband," said Jake.

"I brought extra snacks for energy," said Will. "This is going to be the best field day ever!"

Fergus and Zeke were excited, too. They were as ready as two mice can be.

When the children lined up for field day, Fergus and Zeke sneaked out of their cage and lined up, too.

Ms. Khan was already outside when the class arrived on the playground. She had all the events set up.

"Let's start with the limbo contest!" she said.

Jake bent backward and wiggled under the bar. Will went next. Then Emma.

After every round, the bar got lower and lower.

"How low can you go?" Lucy and Abby chanted. "How low can you go?"

Fergus and Zeke went under the bar over and over. It wasn't very challenging.

"We are talented at limbo," said Fergus.
"I didn't even have to bend."

"We are not talented," said Zeke. "We are
short. Let's find a more exciting event."

The fifty-yard dash was about to begin, so Fergus and Zeke hurried to the starting line.

"I am feeling fast!" said Zeke.

"I am feeling small," said Fergus. "Are you sure this is a good idea?"

Before Zeke could answer, Ms. Khan called out, "On your marks . . . get set . . . go!"

"This event is a little too exciting for me,"
said Fergus. "We're about to get trampled!"

"Let's try something else," said Zeke.

Fergus and Zeke tried everything.

But the Hula-Hoops were too big

for mice.

The water balloons were too heavy

to toss.

The high jump was totally out of reach.

And kickball was absolutely terrifying.

"We thought we were so fast and strong," said Fergus. "But these are not mouse-size events."

"We *are* fast and strong," said Zeke. "We are also clever. We can set up our own field day!"

CHAPTER 3
TUG-OF-MOUSE

Fergus and Zeke found an open space near the woods. They gathered some sticks, set them up to make a bar, and made a pillow of leaves on one side.

"Hooray!" said Fergus. "Now we have a mouse-size high jump!"

"I wish we had mouse-size water balloons to toss," said Zeke.

"We have acorns," said Fergus.

"That works," said Zeke. They took turns throwing them to each other and then tried to see who could throw them the farthest. Zeke was very good at that. "Look how strong I am!" he said. He threw the acorn so far that it  flew right over Fergus's head and into the high-jump area.

Fergus made a Hula-Hoop out of a bendy bracelet someone left behind on the playground. And Zeke found a sturdy vine to use for tug-of-war.

They tugged back and forth, back and forth, until Fergus saw something that caught his attention.

SPLASH!

"I won!" said Zeke.

"Yes, you did," said Fergus. "But look!"

He pointed to the playground. The children had made a circle around Ms. Khan's big rainbow parachute. When they held the edges and raised their arms over their heads, the parachute puffed up into a big, billowing balloon.

"Now sneak inside and tuck in the edges behind you!" Ms. Khan said.

The children scrambled to hide underneath.

"That looks like so much fun." Zeke sighed. "I wish we could play, too."

Just then, an old shopping bag blew past in the wind. Fergus grabbed it and smiled.

"We *can* play!" he said. "I just found a parachute."

"That is not a parachute," said Zeke. "That is a bag."

"It can be a parachute if we use our imaginations," said Fergus. "Hold it up high!"

So Fergus and Zeke sat on opposite sides of their parachute. They lifted it way up in the air so it billowed out above them. Then they sneaked inside and tucked the edges in behind them.

It was like having a campout inside the sun.

"I love our parachute," said Fergus.

"Me, too," said Zeke. "But I am getting hungry. Do you think it's almost time for ice pops?"

"Maybe," Fergus said. He listened carefully to see if he could hear Miss Maxwell's class lining up. But the playground sounded very, very quiet.

Too quiet.

When Fergus and Zeke peeked out from under their parachute, everyone was gone.

"Oh no! The school doors are closed," said Fergus. "How will we get back to Miss Maxwell's room?"

"I don't know," said Zeke. "But I want my ice pop. We have to find a way."

CHAPTER 4
LOCKED OUT

Fergus and Zeke ran around the school looking for a way in. But the only open window was on the second floor. They couldn't jump that high.

"That window is too high for jumping," said Zeke. "But it's not too high for throwing. Remember how strong I am?"

"You are pretty strong," said Fergus. "Are you going to throw acorns in the window?"

"No," said Zeke. "I am going to throw you."

Fergus did not think that was the best idea. But he curled up as small as he could and let Zeke pick him up.

"Ready?" asked Zeke.

Fergus did not feel ready.

Zeke counted, "One . . . two . . . three!"

But before Zeke could throw Fergus, he lost his balance, tipped backward, and dropped him.

Whumpf!

"Ow!" said Fergus.

"I'm sorry," said Zeke. "You are heavier than an acorn."

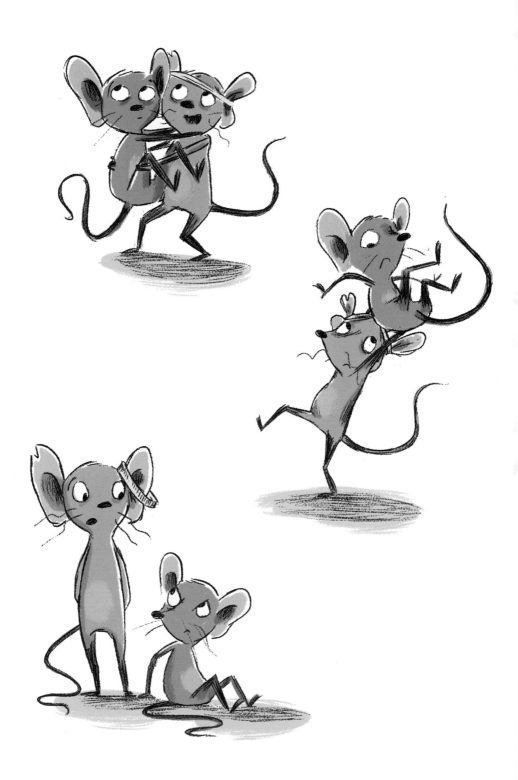

Fergus looked up at the high window. Then he looked at the trees and the jungle gym. "We have tried jumping and throwing," he said, "but we have not tried climbing. And mice are especially good at that."

Fergus and Zeke ran to the jungle gym.

They shimmied up the monkey bars and balanced along the top.

Then they jumped to a tree branch. They climbed higher and higher.

"Look!" Fergus pointed to the open window. "That is Miss Maxwell's classroom. I see Emma!"

But Emma did not see Fergus and Zeke.

"Our tree is too far away," said Fergus. He pointed to another tree with a branch right above the window. "That is where we need to be."

"I could throw you over," Zeke said.

"I do not think that is a good idea," said Fergus. "We need a better plan."

"What we need," Zeke said, "is a zip line!" He fastened their Hula-Hoop around a telephone wire. "Grab on!"

They took a deep breath and jumped.

"Woo-hoo!" Zeke shouted. "I see the playground and the soccer field!"

"I see that we are about to crash," said Fergus. "Look out!"

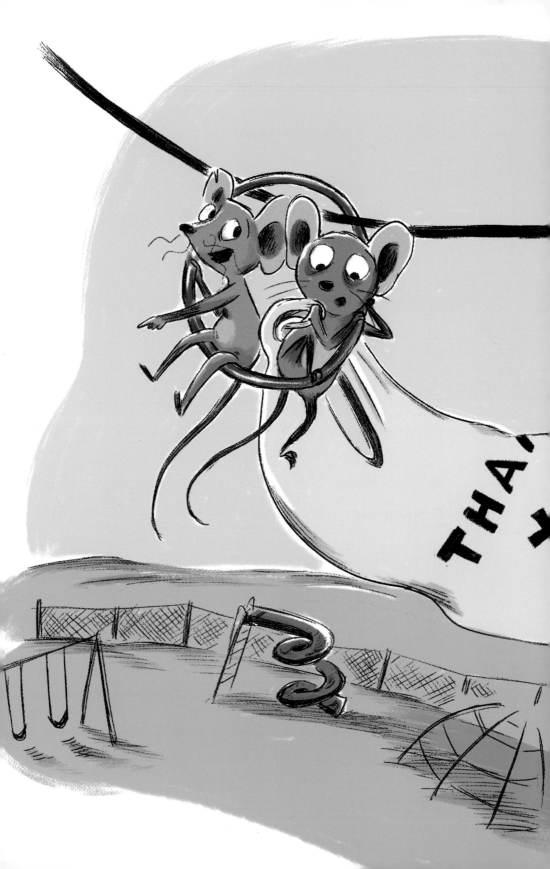

Just in time, they reached out and caught a tree branch above Miss Maxwell's windowsill.

"Now we just have to jump," Zeke said.

Fergus looked down from the branch. Way, way down.

"Don't worry," said Zeke. "We have a parachute!"

Fergus and Zeke lifted their parachute up high. "Ready?" said Fergus.

"Ready!" said Zeke.

They jumped — and landed gently on Miss Maxwell's windowsill.

But the window was only open a crack. Could they fit through the gap?

"Oh no!" cried Zeke. "Now we will never get our ice pops!"

Fergus looked through the window. He saw the children laughing and slurping and having fun.

"We can still fit!" Fergus said. "We just have to do the limbo!"

Fergus and Zeke bent backward as far as they could. Then they wiggled and scooted forward.

"How low can you go, Zeke?" Fergus called out. "How low can you go?"

"Low enough for an ice pop!" Zeke said as they hopped down. "We did it!"

"Look, Miss Maxwell!" Emma called. "The mice got out!"

"Oh dear." Miss Maxwell hurried over. Gently, she lifted Fergus and Zeke back into their cage.

Fergus had never been so happy to see the spinny wheel.

"That was fun!" said Zeke. "I can't wait for next year's field day!"

"Yes," said Fergus. "But maybe next year, we can have field day right here."